Oona

For my editor, Mabel Hsu, who is sweet and a little bit salty. Thank you. —K.D.

For family, friends, and everyone else who provided love, patience, and support while I strived toward making my dreams a reality. —R.F.

Katherine Tegen Books is an imprint of HarperCollins Publishers.

Oona
Text copyright © 2021 by Kelly DiPucchio
Illustrations copyright © 2021 by Raissa Figueroa
All rights reserved. Printed in the United States of America.

ISBN 978-0-06-298224-7

The artist used Procreate to create the digital illustrations for this book.
Typography and lettering by Molly Fehr
20 21 22 23 24 PC 10 9 8 7 6 5 4 3
First Edition

Oona

words by
Kelly DiPucchio

pictures by
Raissa Figueroa

KT KATHERINE TEGEN BOOKS
An Imprint of HarperCollinsPublishers

Oona was sweet . . .
. . . and a little bit salty, like
the ocean where she lived.

She was also brave and curious,
like most treasure hunters.

When Oona was just a baby (no bigger than a scallop),
she chased a pearl into the mouth of a whale!

Lucky for her . . .

. . . she popped
right . . .
back . . .
out.

As the years passed, Oona
found bigger treasure . . .
. . . and even bigger trouble.
It's a good thing she has Otto.

Oona rescued Otto from an oyster net when he was just a pup. She taught him tricks, like . . .

Sit.

Roll Over.

Walrus.

And her favorite—
Pufferfish!

Oona and Otto searched for treasure nearly every day.
They uncovered keys and coins and buttons and bottles.
Sometimes they even found lost gold!

And sometimes . . .
lost glasses

But there was one special treasure
Oona could never quite reach.

The crown.

It was extra sparkly in a way that made Oona's heart thump. But the crown was stuck deep in the rift, and not a pole, or a pail, or the sticky stick of a snail could get it unstuck.

Still, Oona was determined.

Her next plan was a good one. She'd knock the crown loose. Unfortunately, the current *shifted*. The lobster crate and rock *drifted*. And the squid . . . well, see for yourself.

It's hard to say who was more surprised when the water cleared,

Oona or the shark.

Her third plan most *definitely* would have worked if the crabs hadn't been so crabby and the waves hadn't been so wavy.

And if that *loooong* ship plank hadn't bumped her head (hard!) before the greedy, greedy rift gobbled *it* up too.

Poor Oona. This was getting personal.

She shouted into the pit, "You can keep your dumb crown. I quit!"

Generally speaking, mermaids are not quitters. But at this point, one could hardly blame her.

Instead of looking for treasure with Otto, Oona napped on the rocks with the sea lions.

She drew pictures in the sand with the starfish.

And she read from her favorite glass bottles with her land friends.

All of this would have been perfectly fine, except Oona wasn't perfectly fine. Clearly, she was missing her spark, and a mermaid without her spark is like a seagull without an appetite.

Unnatural.

A seashell washed ashore.
Oona studied it thoughtfully.
It gave her an idea.

She got right to work.

The next day Oona peered nervously into the rift.

Why did it look so much deeper and scarier than she remembered?

Otto pretended to be a narwhal, making Oona laugh. Admittedly, the new treasure-hunting goggles she'd invented were funny-looking, but they were also her best shot at reaching the crown.

She dove to the bottom
of the murky rift. That's when Oona
noticed something she couldn't see from above.

A bridge.

A bridge made from a crate. A rock. And the very
same plank that had plunked her on the head!

And it led straight to the crown.

But what was that rumbling sound?
It grew louder. *And louder!*

The ocean floor shook and the water around Oona churned into
a thick stew of swirling sand and sea creatures. She couldn't see!
She felt trapped!

Would the hungry rift gobble her up too?

Through the commotion Oona could hear something else in the distance. It was faint but comforting and familiar.

The whales.

Oona sang along until the rumbling stopped and the water cleared. Finally! This was her chance! Oona held her breath.

Ready? Steady.

AIM!

Clink!

"We did it!" Oona cheered, placing the crown on her best friend.

"It really is beautiful," she gushed.

"BUT THESE!" Oona said excitedly,
holding up her new goggles.
"These are spectacular!"

Otto agreed.

Because sometimes the best treasure in the world isn't found.

It's made.